Winnie-the-Pooh's
Friendship Book

A. A. MILNE

Winnie-the-Pooh's Friendship Book

WITH DECORATIONS BY
ERNEST H. SHEPARD

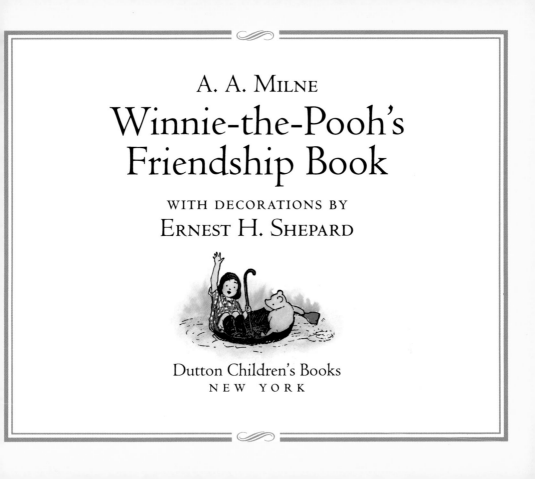

Dutton Children's Books
NEW YORK

Published in the United States by Dutton Children's Books,
a division of Penguin Books USA Inc.
375 Hudson Street, New York, New York 10014

Designed by Joseph Rutt

Printed in Hong Kong
First Edition
10 9 8 7 6 5 4 3 2 1
ISBN 0-525-45204-4

Us Two

Wherever I am, there's always Pooh,
There's always Pooh and Me.
Whatever I do, he wants to do,
"Where are you going today?" says Pooh:
"Well, that's very odd 'cos I was too.
Let's go together," says Pooh, says he.
"Let's go together," says Pooh.

Now We Are Six

Walking in the Wind

"Let's go and see *everybody*," said Pooh. "Because when you've been walking in the wind for miles, and you suddenly go into somebody's house, and he says, 'Hallo, Pooh, you're just in time for a little smackerel of something,' and you are, then it's what I call a Friendly Day."

The House At Pooh Corner

A Place to Call Home

"If your own house is blown down, you *must* go
somewhere else, mustn't you, Piglet? What would *you*
do, if *your* house was blown down?"

Before Piglet could think, Pooh answered for him.

"He'd come and live with me," said Pooh, "wouldn't
you, Piglet?"

Piglet squeezed his paw.

"Thank you, Pooh," he said, "I should love to."

The House At Pooh Corner

At Rabbit's Doorway

"Well, could you very kindly tell me where Rabbit is?"

"He has gone to see his friend Pooh Bear, who is a great friend of his."

"But this *is* Me!" said Bear, very much surprised.

"What sort of Me?"

"Pooh Bear."

"Are you sure?" said Rabbit, still more surprised.

"Quite, quite sure," said Pooh.

"Oh, well, then, come in."

Winnie-the-Pooh

Getting Pooh Unstuck

So he took hold of Pooh's front paws and Rabbit took hold of Christopher Robin, and all Rabbit's friends and relations took hold of Rabbit, and they all pulled together. . . .

Winnie-the-Pooh

Puppy and I

I met a Puppy as I went walking;
We got talking,
Puppy and I.
"Where are you going this nice fine day?"
(I said to the Puppy as he went by).
"Up in the hills to roll and play."
"*I'll* come with you, Puppy," said I.

When We Were Very Young

Playing

Kanga said, "Now then, run along."

"Where shall we run along to?" asked Roo.

"You can go and collect some fir-cones for me," said Kanga, giving them a basket.

So they went to the Six Pine Trees, and threw fir-cones at each other until they had forgotten what they came for, and they left the basket under the trees and went back to dinner.

The House At Pooh Corner

A Very Helpful Bear

Pooh felt that he ought to say something helpful about it, but didn't quite know what. So he decided to do something helpful instead.

"Eeyore," he said solemnly, "I, Winnie-the-Pooh, will find your tail for you."

"Thank you, Pooh," answered Eeyore. "You're a real friend," said he. "Not like Some," he said.

Winnie-the-Pooh

The Expotition

In a little while they were all ready at the top of the Forest, and the Expotition started. First came Christopher Robin and Rabbit, then Piglet and Pooh; then Kanga, with Roo in her pocket, and Owl; then Eeyore; and, at the end, in a long line, all Rabbit's friends-and-relations.

"I didn't ask them," explained Rabbit carelessly. "They just came. They always do. They can march at the end, after Eeyore."

Winnie-the-Pooh

Buttercup Days

Where is Anne?
  Head above the buttercups,
Walking by the stream,
  Down among the buttercups.
Where is Anne?
Walking with her man,
Lost in a dream,
  Lost among the buttercups.

What has she got in that little brown head?
Wonderful thoughts which can never be said.
What has she got in that firm little fist of hers?
Somebody's thumb, and it feels like Christopher's.

Where is Anne?
Close to her man.
Brown head, gold head,
   In and out the buttercups.
   Now We Are Six

Eeyore

"I might have known," said Eeyore. "After all, one can't complain. I have my friends. Somebody spoke to me only yesterday. And was it last week or the week before that Rabbit bumped into me and said 'Bother!' The Social Round. Always something going on."

Winnie-the-Pooh

The Bunch of Violets

Piglet had got up early that morning to pick himself
a bunch of violets; and when he had picked them
and put them in a pot in the middle of his house, it
suddenly came over him that nobody had ever picked
Eeyore a bunch of violets, and the more he thought of
this, the more he thought how sad it was to be an
Animal who had never had a bunch of violets picked
for him. So he hurried out again, saying to himself,
"Eeyore, Violets," and then "Violets, Eeyore," in case
he forgot, because it was that sort of day, and he
picked a large bunch and trotted along, smelling them,
and feeling very happy, until he came to the place
where Eeyore was.

The House At Pooh Corner

The Search for Small

"Have you seen Small anywhere about?"

"I don't think so," said Pooh. And then, after thinking a little more, he said: "Who is Small?"

"One of my friends-and-relations," said Rabbit carelessly.

This didn't help Pooh much, because Rabbit had so many friends-and-relations, and of such different sorts and sizes, that he didn't know whether he ought to be looking for Small at the top of an oak-tree or in the petal of a buttercup.

The House At Pooh Corner

Piglet and the Flood

"If only," he thought, as he looked out of the window, "I had been in Pooh's house, or Christopher Robin's house, or Rabbit's house when it began to rain, then I should have had Company all this time, instead of being here all alone, with nothing to do except wonder when it will stop." And he imagined himself with Pooh, saying, "Did you ever see such rain, Pooh?" and Pooh saying, "Isn't it *awful*, Piglet?" and Piglet saying, "I wonder how it is over Christopher Robin's way" and Pooh saying, "I should think poor old Rabbit is about flooded out by this time." It would have been jolly to talk like this, and really, it wasn't much good having anything exciting like floods, if you couldn't share them with somebody.

Winnie-the-Pooh

Binker

Binker—what I call him—is a secret of my own,
And Binker is the reason why I never feel alone.
Playing in the nursery, sitting on the stair,
Whatever I am busy at, Binker will be there.

Binker isn't greedy, but he does like things to eat,
So I have to say to people when they're giving
    me a sweet,
"Oh, Binker wants a chocolate, so could you give
    me two?"
And then I eat it for him, 'cos his teeth are rather
    new.

Now We Are Six

Reassurance

Piglet sidled up to Pooh from behind.

"Pooh!" he whispered.

"Yes, Piglet?"

"Nothing," said Piglet, taking Pooh's paw. "I just wanted to be sure of you."

The House At Pooh Corner

Talking

At first as they stumped along the path which edged the Hundred Acre Wood, they didn't say much to each other; but when they came to the stream and had helped each other across the stepping stones, and were able to walk side by side again over the heather, they began to talk in a friendly way about this and that, and Piglet said, "If you see what I mean, Pooh," and Pooh said, "It's just what I think myself, Piglet," and Piglet said, "But, on the other hand, Pooh, we must remember," and Pooh said, "Quite true, Piglet, although I had forgotten it for the moment."

Winnie-the-Pooh

The Morning Walk

When Anne and I go out a walk,
We hold each other's hand and talk
Of all the things we mean to do
When Anne and I are forty-two.

And when we've thought about a thing,
Like bowling hoops or bicycling,
Or falling down on Anne's balloon,
We do it in the afternoon.

Now We Are Six

The Best Thing

"What do you like doing best in the world, Pooh?" asked Christopher Robin.

"What I like best in the whole world is Me and Piglet going to see You, and You saying 'What about a little something?' and Me saying, 'Well, I shouldn't mind a little something, should you, Piglet,' and it being a hummy sort of day outside, and birds singing."

The House At Pooh Corner

Sand-Between-the-Toes

I went down to the shouting sea,
Taking Christopher down with me,
For Nurse had given us sixpence each—
And down we went to the beach.

> We had sand in the eyes and the ears and
>   the nose,
> And sand in the hair, and sand-between-
>   the-toes.
> Whenever a good nor' wester blows,
> Christopher is certain of
> Sand-between-the-toes.

When We Were Very Young

Promises

"Pooh, *promise* you won't forget about me, ever.
Not even when I'm a hundred."
Pooh thought for a little.
"How old shall *I* be then?"
"Ninety-nine."
Pooh nodded.
"I promise," he said.

The House At Pooh Corner

Friends Forever

So they went off together. But wherever they go, and whatever happens to them on the way, in that enchanted place on the top of the Forest, a little boy and his Bear will always be playing.

The House At Pooh Corner